Sony Pictures
Animation
presents

THE STAR™

They Followed the Star

SIMON SPOTLIGHT

New York London Toronto Sydney New Delhi

SIMON SPOTLIGHT

An imprint of Simon & Schuster Children's Publishing Division

1230 Avenue of the Americas, New York, New York 10020

This Simon Spotlight paperback edition October 2017

TM & © 2017 Sony Pictures Animation Inc. All Rights Reserved.

For information about special discounts for bulk purchases, please contact
Simon & Schuster Special Sales at 1-866-506-1949 or
business@simonandschuster.com.

Manufactured in the United States of America 0917 CWM

10 9 8 7 6 5 4 3 2 1

ISBN 978-1-5344-1480-8 (pbk)

ISBN 978-1-5344-1481-5 (eBook)

One night a new star appeared in the sky. Everyone looked up in awe.

Animals everywhere saw the Star and wondered what it meant. A small donkey named Bo knew the Star was important.

"Whoa," said Bo. "This doesn't happen every day.
That Star means something special is coming!"

As the months passed, the Star grew bigger and brighter. The animals watched its progress in the sky. Some, like a trio of camels carrying three great wise men, traveled a long distance to follow the Star.

Bo hit the road as well. He and his friends Dave, the dove, and Ruth, the sheep, were helping a young couple named Mary and Joseph who were traveling from Nazareth to Bethlehem. Mary was going to have a baby, and some days it was very hard for her to travel, so Bo helped out any way he could.

There were other travelers, too. When King Herod heard that the Star meant a new king would be born, he sent a hunter after Mary and Joseph. King Herod was a mean, jealous man. No one would be king except him, especially not a baby.

Finally, Mary and Joseph made it safe and sound to Bethlehem. But there was no room for them to stay anywhere. They went from inn to inn and were turned away each time. The inns were all full.

Things went from bad to worse, when Bo got separated from his friends. He was taken away and tied up in a strange, dark place. He didn't know what to do. So he prayed.

"God, hello, um. I don't really know if you listen to prayers from donkeys, but I don't know what else to do," said Bo.

Suddenly, Bo heard voices. He realized he was not alone. Bo had been tied up in a manger filled with other animals. All the animals were excited. They showed him how the Star was shining directly down on their manger. Bo saw how beautiful and special the Star was, and asked the animals to help him get free so he could find Mary and Joseph.

In the meantime Dave and Ruth enlisted the help of
animals all over Bethlehem.

Once Bo escaped, he raced away from the Hunter and found Mary and Joseph. He looked up, spotted the Star's bright light, and knew just what to do.

While the animals kept the Hunter away from the manger, something miraculous happened–Mary and Joseph's baby boy was born. They named him Jesus. The three great wise men from the East arrived with gold, frankincense, and myrrh. The wise men told Mary and Joseph the gifts were for the new King— the baby Jesus!

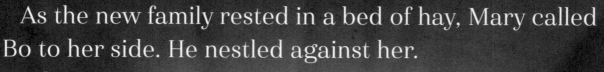

As the new family rested in a bed of hay, Mary called
Bo to her side. He nestled against her.

What a wondrous night! Following the Star had led Bo to
something important—a family.